Pumpkin Fever

Written by Charnan Simon
Illustrated by Jan Bryan-Hunt

Children's Press®
A Division of Scholastic Inc.
New York • Toronto • London • Auckland • Sydney
Mexico City • New Delhi • Hong Kong
Danbury, Connecticut

Dear Parents/Educators,

Welcome to Rookie Ready to Learn. Each Rookie Reader in this series includes additional age-appropriate Let's Learn Together activity pages that help your young child to be better prepared when starting school.

Pumpkin Fever offers opportunities for you and your child to talk about the important social/emotional skill of **natural curiosity**.

Here are early-learning skills you and your child will encounter in the *Pumpkin Fever* Let's Learn Together pages:

• Naming numbers
• Shapes
• Storytelling

We hope you enjoy sharing this delightful, enhanced reading experience with your early learner.

Library of Congress Cataloging-in-Publication Data

Simon, Charnan.
 Pumpkin fever/written by Charnan Simon; illustrated by Jan Bryan-Hunt.
  p. cm. — (Rookie ready to learn)

 Summary: In simple text that teaches about shapes, Erin and her parents buy two wonderful, round pumpkins and while she and her father carve one into a jack-o-lantern, Mom prepares hers a different way. Includes learning activities, parent tips, and word list.

 ISBN 978-0-531-25643-5 (library binding) — ISBN 978-0-531-26803-2 (pbk.)

 [1. Pumpkin—Fiction. 2. Jack-o-lanterns—Fiction. 3. Family life—Fiction. 4. Shape.] I. Bryan-Hunt, Jan, ill. II. Title.

 PZ7.S6035Pum 2011   [E]—dc22   2011010242

Acknowledgments
© 2007 Jan Bryan-Hunt, front and back cover illustrations, pages 3–34, 35 girl, pumpkins, pumpkin patch, 36–38, 39 top jack-o-lantern, 40. © iStockphoto/Thinkstock pages 34 and 38.

1 2 3 4 5 6 7 8 9 10 R 18 17 16 15 14 13 12 11

Erin's family had pumpkin fever.

They went to a big,
square field . . .

4

full of fat, round
pumpkins . . .

and chose the roundest pumpkins of all!

Dad helped Erin carve
her pumpkin.

"Two triangle eyes!" said Erin.

"Mmm," said Mom. "Very nice!"

"One triangle nose!" said Erin.

"Mmm," said Mom. "I like it!"

"One half-circle mouth full of scary, square teeth!" said Erin.

"Mmm," said Mom. "Scary!"

A rectangle candle made Erin's pumpkin perfect.

"Mom!" Erin said. "Don't you want a pumpkin like mine?"

"Mmm," said Mom.
"I love your pumpkin!
But my pumpkin is nice, too!"

"Mmm!" said Erin.

Congratulations!

You just finished reading *Pumpkin Fever* and learned about one girl's trip to a pumpkin patch in fall.

About the Author

Charnan Simon lives in Madison, Wisconsin, where pumpkin fields abound. Her husband and daughters are the carvers in the house, and their pumpkins are sometimes scary, sometimes funny, and always pretty messy.

About the Illustrator

Jan Bryan-Hunt is a freelance illustrator living near Kansas City, Missouri, with her husband and two children. Jan and her family enjoy visiting a local pumpkin patch every fall.

I Love Fall!

A round **pumpkin** grows from a vine.

I pick the **pumpkin** to be mine.

A juicy **apple** so good to eat.

Crunch, my **apple** tastes so sweet!

A colorful **leaf** blows all over town.

I spot **leaf** after **leaf**—red, orange, and brown.

Fall is such a great season;

pumpkins, apples, and leaves are the reason!

Through the Pumpkin Patch

Help Erin find her way through the pumpkin patch. Use your finger to trace her path.

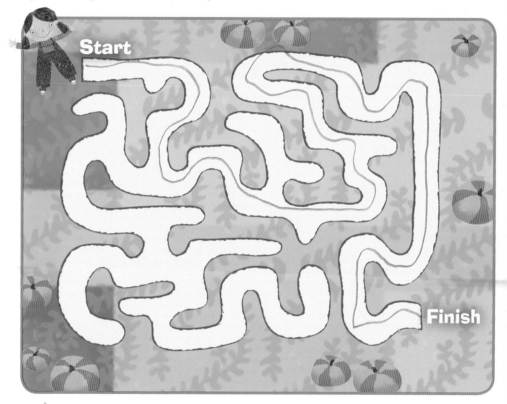

PARENT TIP: After your child has followed the path that will take the girl to the finish, go to page 5 in the story and share the illustration of the pumpkin patch, explaining that the pumpkins grow on vines. Then point to the girl in the middle of the patch and offer this story starter: "One day this little girl decided to search for the best pumpkin in the patch. She…" Invite your child to finish the story. You'll be helping her develop language and creative-thinking skills!

How Many Pumpkins?

The kids in the story are picking pumpkins from the patch.

- Count how many pumpkins are in the picture.

- Next see how many pumpkins each child picked by counting the pumpkins in each box. Point to the number you counted in each box.

- Now see if you can find the rabbit, the bird, and the squirrel hiding in the pumpkin patch.

PARENT TIP: Help your child gain skill in counting and number recognition as you enjoy this activity. Then go back to pages 4 and 5 of the book. For additional counting experience, help your child count *all the people* and *all the animals* on those two pages.

4   3